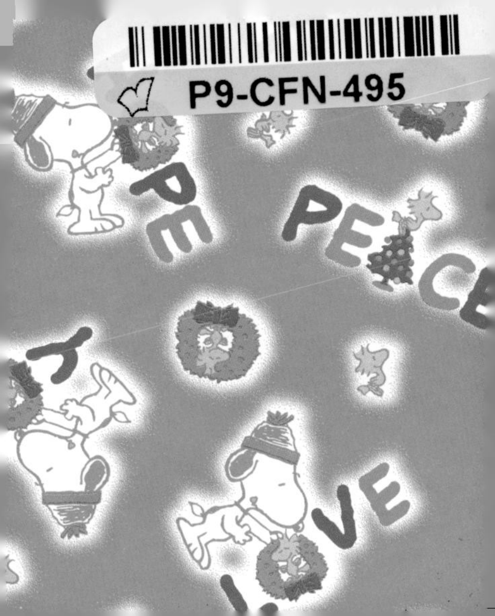

PEANUTS®
A CHARLIE BROWN
CHRISTMAS

It was finally Christmastime, the best time of the year.

The houses were strung with tiny colored lights, their windows shining with the warm yellow glow only Christmas could bring. The scents of pine needles and hot cocoa mingled together,

wafting through the air,
and the sweet sounds of
Christmas carols could
be heard in the distance.

Fluffy white snowflakes
tumbled from the sky onto
a group of joyful children
as they sang and laughed,

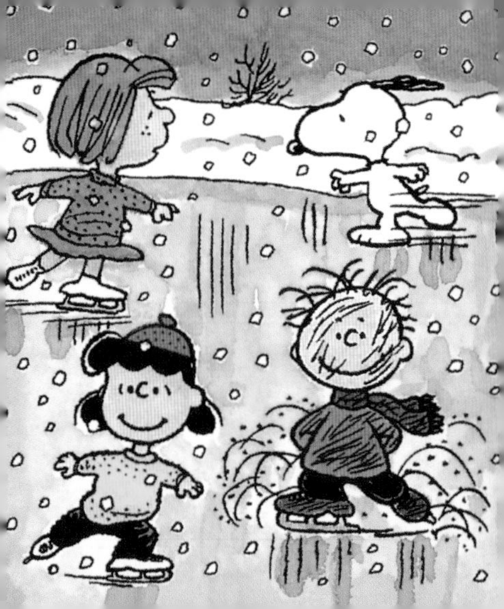

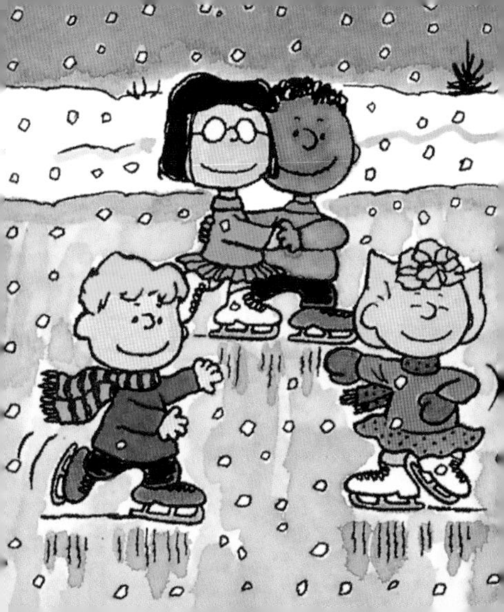

skating on the frozen pond in town. Everyone was happy and full of holiday cheer. That is, everyone except for Charlie Brown.

"I think there must be something wrong with me," he told his friend

Linus. "I just don't under-stand Christmas, I guess.
I might be getting presents
and sending Christmas
cards and decorating trees
and all that, but I'm still
not happy. I don't feel the
way I'm supposed to feel."

Linus looked over at his friend. "Charlie Brown, you're the only person I know who can take a wonderful season like Christmas and turn it into a problem. Maybe Lucy's right. Of all the Charlie

Browns in the world, you're the Charlie Browniest."

Charlie Brown walked through the snow, thinking about what Linus had said. When he reached his mailbox, Charlie Brown hopefully poked his head

inside. It was empty.

"Rats!" he said out loud, feeling sadder than ever.

"Nobody sent me a Christmas card today. I know nobody likes me. Why do we have to have a holiday season to emphasize it?"

Violet was also outside, enjoying the wintry snowfall and reading a holiday card she had just received. "Thanks for the Christmas card you sent me, Violet," said Charlie Brown bitterly.

"I didn't send you a Christmas card," she responded.

Charlie Brown thrust his hands deep in his pockets and made a face. "Don't you know sarcasm when you hear it?"

He walked past the
houses on his street,
and could not help but
notice all his other friends
throwing snowballs,
building snowmen, and
catching snowflakes on
their tongues. Everyone

seemed to be enjoying
themselves, but Charlie
Brown was still sad.

Desperate to discuss
his inappropriate holiday
mood, Charlie Brown sat
down on the stool in front
of Lucy's psychiatric booth.

"I am in sad shape," he told her, frowning. Lucy was excited to have a customer, but she stopped him short before hearing any more details. She demanded that Charlie Brown pay in advance

for her psychiatric advice.
Charlie Brown reached
into his jacket pocket
and dropped a shiny
nickel in her money can.
The coin made a metallic
clinking noise as it fell
to the bottom of the can.

"Boy, I love the beautiful sound of cold, hard cash," said Lucy. "That beautiful, beautiful sound. Nickels, nickels, nickels. That beautiful sound of plunking nickels." Lucy grinned. "Now, what seems to

be your trouble?"

Charlie Brown told her that he knew he should be happy during Christmas, like everyone else, but he just couldn't seem to manage it. Lucy was entirely ready to diagnose his problem.

"Well, as they say on TV, the mere fact that you realize you need help indicates that you are not too far gone." Lucy looked at him sternly. "I think we'd better pinpoint your fears. If we can find out what you're

afraid of, we can label it.
Are you afraid of respon-
sibility? If you are, then you
have hypengyophobia.
How about cats? If you're
afraid of cats, you have
ailurophasia. Are you
afraid of staircases? If

you are, then you have climacaphobia. Maybe you have thalassophobia. This is fear of the ocean, or gephyrobia, which is the fear of crossing bridges. Or maybe you have pantophobia. Do

you think you have panto-
phobia?"

"What's pantophobia?"
asked Charlie Brown.

"The fear of everything,"
she responded.

"That's it!" shouted a
briefly encouraged Charlie

Brown. But then his glum expression returned.

"Actually, Lucy, my trouble is Christmas. I just don't understand it. Instead of feeling happy, I feel sort of let down."

Lucy came around from

behind the booth to con-
front her friend face-to-face.
"You need involvement.
You need to get involved
in some real Christmas
project. How would you
like to be the director
of our Christmas play?"

Charlie Brown could hardly believe his ears. "Me? You want me to be the director of the Christmas play?"

Lucy tried hard to persuade Charlie Brown to join in. "Sure, Charlie Brown. We need a director.

We've got a shepherd,
musicians, animals, everyone we need. We've even
got a Christmas Queen."

Charlie Brown hesitated.
What did he know about
how to properly direct
a Christmas play? "Don't

worry," Lucy reassured him. "I'll be there to help you."

Charlie Brown thought for a moment. Maybe he did need to get involved with a holiday project in order to feel better about things. Lucy's confidence was almost contagious. Besides, he couldn't let everyone down. They needed him. Figuring he had nothing to lose, Charlie Brown agreed to meet Lucy and the rest of the cast later at the auditorium.

"Incidentally," Lucy added, "I know how you feel about all this Christmas business, getting depressed and all that. It happens to me every year. I never get what I really want. I always get a lot of stupid toys or a bicycle or clothes or something like that.

"What is it you want?" asked Charlie Brown.

Lucy looked right at him. "Real estate."

Just then, Charlie Brown noticed his dog, Snoopy, pass by, hauling a large brown box overflowing with colorful holiday lights and decorations. He followed Snoopy back to his doghouse and watched as the dog began to create a large display of ornaments and lights on the roof. "What's going on here?" he inquired. Snoopy grinned and hand-ed him a flyer. It said:

FIND THE TRUE
MEANING OF
CHRISTMAS.
WIN MONEY,
MONEY, MONEY!

SPECTACULAR,

SUPERCOLOSSAL,

NEIGHBORHOOD

CHRISTMAS LIGHTS

AND DISPLAY CONTEST!

Charlie Brown looked up at the sky in dismay. Even his very own dog had gone commercial! The thought of the contest made Charlie Brown feel positively sick. Was money all anyone cared about? Charlie

Brown couldn't stand it. He threw the flyer in the air and left Snoopy to decorate his doghouse alone.

As he walked away, Charlie Brown ran into his little sister, Sally. "I've been looking for you, big brother," she said. "Will you please write a letter to Santa Claus for me? You write it and I'll tell you what I want to say." Charlie Brown was in a hurry to get to the school auditorium on time for

play rehearsal, but he couldn't say no to his sister. Charlie Brown took the pen and clipboard from Sally's outstretched hands and prepared to write.

"Okay, shoot," he said.

Sally began to rattle off

her letter to Santa. "I have been extra good this year, so I have a long list of presents that I want."

"Oh, brother," sighed Charlie Brown.

Sally continued. "Please note the size and color of

each item and send as many as possible. If it seems too complicated, make it easy on yourself. Just send money. How about tens and twenties?"

Charlie Brown was dismayed. Even his baby

sister had become greedy. Writing a letter to Santa Claus was one thing, but demanding cash from him was just absurd.

Charlie Brown returned the pen and clipboard to his sister and hurried to the auditorium for the first day of rehearsal. He arrived just on time, and the rest of the kids were already gathered onstage and in the wings of the theater. He walked over to the director's chair

to address the cast, but
as he began to speak,
Charlie Brown realized
that all the kids were
dancing and goofing
around, and that no one
was paying any attention
to him at all.

He picked up a mega-
phone and tried again.
"All right," he said. "Stop
the music. We're going
to do this play and we're
going to do it right."

Lucy picked up a stack
of scripts and began to

assign roles. Freida played the innkeeper's wife, Pig Pen played the innkeeper, and Shermy played a shepherd. Snoopy was delighted to play the roles of all the different animals, from sheep, to cow, to penguin.

When she came around to Linus, who was also playing a shepherd, Lucy handed him his script and instructed him to memorize his lines so he could recite them on cue. Linus hugged his trusty blue blanket and began to protest. "This is ridiculous! I can't memorize something like this so quickly. Why should I be put through such agony? Give me one good reason why I should have to memorize this!"

Lucy glowered at Linus and made a fist, curling one menacing finger at a time. "I'll give you five good reasons," she said. "One, two, three, four, five!"

Linus stared at Lucy's threatening fist, and swallowed hard. "Those are good reasons," he agreed. "Christmas is not only getting too commercial, it's getting too dangerous!"

Lucy frowned. "And get rid of that stupid blanket. What's a Christmas shep-

herd going to look like holding a stupid blanket like that?"

Charlie Brown did his best to control his temper. "All right. Let's have it quiet," he said. "Places, everybody. Schroeder, set the mood for the first scene." Schroeder sat at his piano and began to play a cheerful jazz tune. The entire cast started to dance all over the place. "Cut! Cut!" shouted Charlie Brown. It was all wrong.

He suggested that they rehearse another scene instead. But no one seemed to be able to concentrate. Freida complained that Pig Pen's dust was ruining the style of her naturally curly hair. Sally stayed

close to Linus, watching his every move, and occasionally resting her little blonde head on his shoulder. "Isn't he the cutest thing?" she asked anyone who would listen. Meanwhile, Lucy and Snoopy demanded a lunch break.

"Good grief,"
exclaimed Charlie Brown,
who was determined to
get back to work on the
play. "There's no time for
foolishness. Let's take it
from the top again."

Schroeder began to play his jazzy piano music again, which sent everyone into another dancing frenzy.

Lucy came over and stood next to Charlie Brown. "What's the matter?" she asked. "Don't you think it's great?" Charlie Brown shook his head. Something just wasn't right. "Look," said Lucy matter-of-factly, "Let's face it. We all know that Christmas is a big

commercial racket. It's run
by a big eastern syndicate,
you know."

"Well," Charlie Brown
responded, "this is one
play that's not going to
be commercial. What
our play needs is the

proper Christmas mood.
We need a Christmas tree."

Lucy clapped her hands.
"Hey, perhaps a tree. A
great, big, shiny, aluminum
Christmas tree! That's it!
Get the biggest aluminum
tree you can find. Maybe

paint it pink!"

Charlie Brown left Lucy
in charge of rehearsal,
and set out with Linus
to find the perfect tree
for their play. The boys
finally reached a Christmas
tree lot filled with a vast

array of bright, shiny, aluminum trees. Then, in the midst of all the brightly-colored metal, they caught sight of a tiny green pine tree on a simple wooden stand. "Gee," said Linus, "I didn't know they still made wooden Christmas trees."

Charlie Brown went over to the little tree. "This one seems to need a home," he said.

Linus stopped him for a moment. "I don't know.

Remember what Lucy said? This doesn't seem to fit the modern spirit."

But Charlie Brown was adamant. "I don't care," he said. "We'll decorate it and it will be just right for our play. Besides, I

think it needs me."

They returned to the auditorium, and Charlie Brown carefully placed the little green Christmas tree on top of Schroeder's piano. "We're back," he announced, getting everyone's attention.

All the kids gathered around the small, sad-looking tree. "Boy, are you stupid, Charlie Brown," said Violet.

Lucy spoke up next. "You were supposed to get a

good tree. Can't you even tell a good tree from a poor tree?"

"You're hopeless, Charlie Brown," sighed Patty.

"You've been dumb before. But this time, you really did it," said Lucy.

All of the kids laughed
at Charlie Brown and
at his pathetic little tree.
Then they all walked
away, leaving him alone
and bewildered next to
the piano. Linus approached
him slowly, blanket in hand.

"I guess you were right, Linus," said Charlie Brown miserably. "I shouldn't have picked this little tree. Everything I do turns into a disaster. I guess I really don't know what Christmas is about. Isn't there anyone who understands what Christmas is all about?"

"Sure," said Linus. "I can tell you what Christmas is all about." He walked to the center of the stage where a single spotlight shone right on him, and he began to speak.

"And there were in the same country shepherds abiding in the field, keeping watch over their flock by night. And lo, the angel of the Lord came upon them, and the glory of the Lord

shone round about them.
And they were sore afraid.
And the angel said unto
them, 'Fear not, for behold,
I bring you tidings of great
joy which will be to all
people. For unto you is
born this day in the city

of David a savior, which is
Christ the Lord. And this
shall be a sign unto you.
Ye shall find the babe
wrapped in swaddling
clothes lying in a manger.'
And suddenly there was
with the angel a multitude

of the heavenly host, praising God and saying, 'Glory to God in the highest, and on Earth peace, goodwill toward men.'"

Linus picked up his blanket and walked back toward the piano. "That's what Christmas is all about, Charlie Brown."

All of the kids in the auditorium were silent. Charlie Brown picked up his little Christmas tree and smiled. He carried it outside and looked up into the dark night sky, twinkling with a million silvery stars.

"Linus is right," he said to himself, the words still echoing in his mind. "I won't let all this commercialism ruin my Christmas.

I'll take this little tree home and decorate it and I'll show them it really will work in our play." He headed home, and came upon Snoopy's prizewinning doghouse. Charlie Brown

grabbed a large red orna-
ment from the roof and
hung it carefully on the
top branch of his little
Christmas tree.

Charlie Brown cringed
with dismay as the entire
tree bent over from the

weight of the single orna-
ment. "I've killed it," he
shouted, feeling sad and
frustrated. "Everything
I touch gets ruined!" He
gave up on decorating
the tree, and walked
away with his shoulders

as bent as the little tree's trunk.

The rest of Charlie Brown's friends walked over to the tree. Linus leaned over and straightened out the branch. "I never thought it was such a bad little tree," he con-

fessed, wrapping his blanket gently around the base of th trunk. "It's not bad at all, really. Maybe it just needs a little love."

The kids looked at Snoopy': doghouse decorations and then at the tree. Without

another word, they
removed the decorations
from the doghouse and
gathered around the sad
little tree. Working together, they quickly
transformed it into a truly
beautiful sight, complete

with a star on top.

Even Lucy had to admit that it looked wonderful. "Charlie Brown is a block-head, but he did get a nice tree."

The whole gang circled around the decorated

tree, and someone began to hum "O, Little Town of Bethlehem." Charlie Brown heard the noise and came over to the group.

"What's going on here?" he asked.

"Merry Christmas,

Charlie Brown!" everyone
shouted. Charlie Brown
couldn't help but smile.
He caught sight of
the tree—his little tree
that no one had wanted—
and he could hardly
believe his eyes.

His friends' efforts had transformed it into something truly special. Everyone sang:

Hark, the herald
angels sing,
Glory to the new-
born King!

Peace on Earth

and mercy mild,

God and sinner

reconciled.

Joyful, all ye

nations rise!

Join the triumph

of the skies!

With angelic

host proclaim:

Christ is born in

Bethlehem.

Hark, the herald
angels sing,
Glory to the new-
born King!

Surrounded by his friends, Charlie Brown realized that Linus had been right about the true meaning of Christmas. This was the Christmas spirit he had been looking for all along.

At last, the season seemed a hundred times brighter, and for Charlie Brown it was truly the merriest Christmas ever.

This book has been bound using
handcraft methods and Smyth-sewn
to ensure durability.

By Charles M. Schulz.

Art adapted by Peter and Nick LoBianco.

The dust jacket and interior were
designed by Corinda Cook.

The text was adapted by Caroline Dolan
from the television special produced
by Lee Mendelson and Bill Melendez.

The text was edited by Andra Serlin
and Heather Orosco.

The text was set in Chuck Font
and Sassoon Infant.